This Storybook Belongs To

Princess_____

Dreams Under the Sea

ADVANCE
PUBLISHERS

Ariel's secret grotto was her favorite place in the undersea world, especially now that the statue of Prince Eric was there.

"Ariel!" cried Sebastian. "Be reasonable. That's not a human; he's nothing but a hunk of rock!"

Ariel put her ear up to the statue's mouth. "He said that if you two would please excuse us for a moment," Ariel announced, "he has something he'd like to say to me alone. Go on, Sebastian. Shoo!"

Ariel placed her head on the statue's shoulder and pretended to answer his proposal. "Why, yes, I'd love to marry you, Eric."

"Marry?" Sebastian roared as he swam back into the grotto. "You will do no such thing. In the name of his royal highness, King Triton, I forbid this kind of talk."

"Hey, Sebastian," Ariel said, "it's a statue, remember? I'm just playing make-believe. Please don't tell my father, okay?"

Sebastian reluctantly shook his head. "I just know I'm going to regret this," he moaned.

"We can have the wedding right here in the grotto," Ariel said. "There's so much to do! You'll both help me, won't you?"

"Help you with what?" Sebastian asked as Ariel showered him with decorations. "It's make-believe. You said so yourself."

"Oh, dream weddings are every bit as much work as real weddings," Ariel said. "Everything has to be just perfect!"

"I think Prince Eric is dressed perfectly for a wedding in this outfit," Ariel said.

"This will never work! The real Prince Eric is human," Sebastian said. "He lives on land! And every self-respecting sea dweller knows that mermaids LIVE UNDERWATER!"

"That may be true," said Ariel. "But who knows what the future will bring...?"

"May I be the chef?" Flounder asked. "Please, please?"

Ariel laughed. "Of course, Flounder," she said. "I want you to prepare all the most wonderful foods you can imagine."

"Seaweed soufflé...plankton pie—" Flounder said happily.

"Oh, yes!" Ariel cried. "And don't forget the wedding cake!"

"Just leave it to me," Flounder said proudly. "This will be a wedding feast like no one has ever seen!"

"Oh, I can hardly wait!" Ariel exclaimed. "I can picture the entire ceremony. My sisters will make such beautiful bridesmaids. And my father will look so proud and distinguished as we—"

"Your father?" Sebastian looked as if he was ready to faint.

"Oh, don't be such a party pooper, Sebastian," Ariel said lightly. "Remember...it's all just pretend."

"I'm leaving," Sebastian said. "I can't take anymore of this nonsense!"

"Flounder," Ariel called. "Sebastian's leaving. Can you think of someone else to be the master conductor of the grand orchestra for the wedding?"

"Grand orchestra?" Sebastian asked.

"Of course *you're* my first choice, Sebastian," Ariel said. "But—"

"'BUT' nothing!" Sebastian cried. "A crab must do what a crab must do. The show—er, rather, the wedding—must go on!"

Grabbing a candlestick, Sebastian began to conduct his pretend orchestra.

"May I have this dance, Ariel?" Flounder asked, bowing politely.

"With pleasure, kind sir!" Ariel laughed. And she and Flounder waltzed and twirled until they were both too dizzy to dance anymore.

That evening in her room, Ariel was trying on her pretend veil when Flounder arrived with a long string of pearls.

"Oh, Flounder, they're beautiful!" Ariel gasped with delight.

"They belong to my friend," Flounder said. "She said you could borrow them."

Now Ariel had something old (the dinglehopper to comb her hair), something new (her veil), something borrowed (the pearls), and something blue (her blue shell bracelet).

"That's everything a bride needs!" Ariel exclaimed.

The next morning, Sebastian scuttled after Ariel as she made her way to the grotto.

"I hope no one sees us," Sebastian said nervously, flailing madly along behind Ariel as she glided from the palace. "It might be hard to explain where you're going dressed like this!"

Flounder was waiting for them outside the entrance to the grotto.

"Are you ready, Ariel?" Flounder
asked as Sebastian scurried past. Ariel
nodded, and Flounder escorted her into
the grotto.
"Dum-dum-de-dum, dum-dum-de-dum...,"
Sebastian was singing as he banged out the wedding march on
an overturned bucket. He stopped abruptly when he caught sight of
Ariel. "Ohhhhhh," wailed Sebastian. "Weddings always make me cry!"

Sebastian cleared his throat importantly. "Do you, Princess Ariel, take this...er...this statue to be your (now listen closely to this part, young lady) MAKE-BELIEVE husband?"

"I do!" Ariel sighed happily.

"And do you, Mr. Pretend Prince, take this perpetually provoking princess to be your make-believe wife?" Sebastian finished.

"He says he does," Ariel said with a giggle.

"Well, then, I suppose I have to pronounce you absolutely 100% IMAGINARY husband and wife," Sebastian said.

"Hooray!" Flounder cheered as he rushed to catch Ariel's bouquet.

With her eyes glowing like stars, Ariel hugged her friends. "Oh, thank you! This has been a wonderful dream wedding!" she cried. "And now I'm inviting you both to my real wedding to Prince Eric. I'm not sure when—or where—or how, but I know it will happen. It won't matter that there's an ocean of difference between us. Nothing can stand in the way of true love."

"Nothing," Flounder agreed dreamily.

Ariel sighed with happiness, imagining a kiss from Eric....
"Ewwwwwwww!" she cried suddenly. She realized that
she was actually kissing a very startled Flounder!

"Ha!" Sebastian shouted. "See what comes of silly notions about marrying human princes...as if that could ever really happen...."